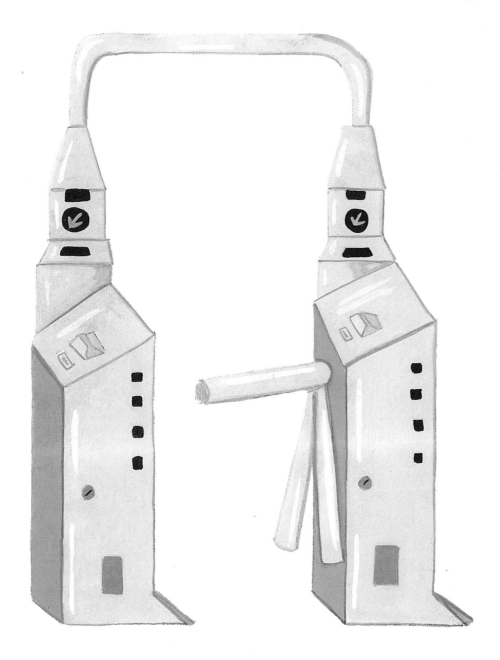

DOWN
in the
SUBWAY

story by
Miriam Cohen

pictures by
Melanie Hope
Greenberg

Star Bright Books
New York

The name Star Bright Books and the logo are trademarks of Star Bright Books, Inc.

Published by Star Bright Books, Inc., New York.

Please visit our website at www.starbrightbooks.com.

Printed in China 9 8 7 6 5 4 3 2

Paperback ISBN: 1-932065-24-5

Hardback ISBN: 1-932065-08-3

Library of Congress Cataloguing in Publication Data is available for this title.

LCCN: 2003042845

To my dearest Gladys, the Island Lady
—M.C.

To Shri Saraswati, the messenger dove
—M.H.G.

It was hot in that subway train. Ohhh, yes! Oscar twirled round and round the pole. Every time he came round, Oscar peeked at the Island Lady.

The Island Lady smiled a fine Islands smile.
"Would you like to know what's in this bag?"
Oscar looked at his mama. He was shy,
don't you see.
His mama smiled. "Yes."

Then the Island Lady reached
down in her bag, and pulled out
. . . the cool blue Island breeze!

"Please, what else is in that bag?"
said Oscar.
The Island Lady reached inside
and pulled out . . . the green
Caribbean Sea!

Oscar ran right in and splashed
and splashed.
Oh, my, he did enjoy that!

Next the Island Lady took out
the picnic lunch from her bag.
Ackee rice, salt fish, the callaloo,
and the soursop soup, guava,
pineapple, and the coconut tarts.
People on the train were just
looking at that food.
The fine smells,
don't you know.

"You must try it now, hear?" said the Island Lady. "There's plenty for all! Yes, indeed! Don't you stop eating now, child! Just leave some crumbs for the little lizards."

"Ummm," said Oscar, and he ate *another* honey-sweet tart. He couldn't help it, don't you see.

"Oh, listen, now! The Calypso Man is coming!"
the Lady said. "That man can make a song
about *anything*!"
Out of the Island Lady's bag jumped
the Calypso Man. He sang,

"Down in the subway.
Down in the subway,
Take the subway va-ca-tion!
Get on at the station,
Look at the people all smilin',
Takin' the trip to the Islands.

"Singin', 'Ackee rice, salt fish, callaloo,
Soursop soup, and the coconut too!'
Once again, mon! 'Ackee rice, salt fish, callaloo,
Soursop soup, and the coconut too!'"

The Calypso Man laughed.
And he jumped right back in the bag.

Now, don't you know, that
Island Lady's bag was wiggling
and bumping?
A whole steel band got
themselves out.

And didn't they play!
Those drums! Walking big like
thunder! And dance-y like little
raindrops on a tin roof.
The Lady was nodding her
head, tapping her toes,
and snapping her fingers.
"This is the jump-up music,"
she told Oscar. "Ohhh, yes!"

She reached in the bag, and pulled out . . .
an Island town! And, don't you know,
everybody in that town started doing
the jump-up!

Well, all those people in the train got so tingly they just *had* to dance.

All the while, the subway train was racketing along the track, shaking with all that fine music and dancing.

"One Hundred Twenty-fifth Street station!" called the conductor.
Now don't you know, that's just where Oscar and his mama and his baby brother had to get off.

The subway train pulled out of the station,
with the Island Lady, cool blue breezes,
green seas, callaloo, and soursop soup,
Calypso Man, steel band, little lizards,
and Island town.
"Good-bye, dear child, good-bye!"
waved the Island Lady.

After that, when Oscar and his mama
and his baby brother went on the subway,
they looked for the Island Lady's train.
But they never did see it again.

"Never mind, honey-sweetie," Oscar's mama said.
His papa said, "I *like* to hear you singing that song."
Well, don't you know, Oscar sang it so much,
pretty soon his baby brother could sing it too.